This book belongs to:

........Isobella........................

Mr. Wrong

EGMONT

We bring stories to life

MR. MEN   **LITTLE MISS**

MR. MEN™ LITTLE MISS™ © THOIP (a Sanrio company)

Mr. Men™ Treasury © 2012 THOIP (a Sanrio company)
Printed and published under licence from Price Stern Sloan, Inc., Los Angeles.
First published in Great Britain 2012
by Egmont UK Limited
The Yellow Building
1 Nicholas Road
London W11 4AN

Mr. Messy © 1972 THOIP (a Sanrio company)
Mr. Muddle © 1976 THOIP (a Sanrio company)
Mr. Bounce © 1976 THOIP (a Sanrio company)
Mr. Lazy © 1976 THOIP (a Sanrio company)
Mr. Worry © 1978 THOIP (a Sanrio company)
Mr. Quiet © 1978 THOIP (a Sanrio company)
Mr. Slow © 1978 THOIP (a Sanrio company)
Mr. Busy © 1978 THOIP (a Sanrio company)
Mr. Wrong © 1978 THOIP (a Sanrio company)

ISBN 978 0 6035 6763 6
52897/1
Printed in China

MR. MEN™

by Roger Hargreaves

TREASURY

Mr. Bounce

Mr. Busy

Mr. Wrong

CONTENTS

Mr. Bounce

MR. WORRY

by Roger Hargreaves

Poor Mr Worry.

Whatever happened, he worried about it.

If it rained, he worried his roof was going to leak.

If it didn't rain, he worried that all the plants in his garden were going to die.

If he set off shopping, he worried that the shops would be shut when he got there.

And when the shops weren't shut when he got there, he worried that he was spending too much money shopping.

And when he got home with his shopping, he worried that he'd left something behind, or that something had fallen out of his basket on the way home.

And when he got home, and discovered that he hadn't left anything behind, and that nothing had fallen out of his basket on the way home, he worried that he'd bought too much.

And then he worried about where to put it all.

Life was just one long worry for poor Mr Worry.

One day, he went for a walk.

He was worried that he might walk too far and not be able to get home, but on the other hand, he was worried that if he didn't walk far enough, he wouldn't get enough exercise.

He hurried along worrying.

Or you could say, he worried along hurrying.

He met Mr Bump.

"I'm very worried about you," he said.

"Why's that?" asked Mr Bump.

"I'm worried that one of these days you might hurt yourself," he said.

"Don't you worry your head about that," replied
Mr Bump.

And went off.

Tripping over his own feet.

Mr Worry went on.

He met Mr Noisy.

"I'm very worried about you," he said.

"Why's that?" asked Mr Noisy.

"I'm worried that you might lose your voice," said Mr Worry.

"Don't you worry your head about that," said Mr Noisy.

And went off.

CLUMP! CLUMP! CLUMP!

Mr Worry went on.

He met Mr Greedy.

"I'm very worried about you," he said.

"Why's that?" asked Mr Greedy.

"I'm worried that you might eat too much and be sick," explained Mr Worry.

"Me?" replied Mr Greedy.

"Eat too much?"

"Impossible!"

And went off.

For lunch.

Mr Worry went on.

He met a wizard.

"Hello," said the wizard. "Who are you?"

"I'm Mr Worry."

"And you look it," commented the wizard.

"Tell you what," he went on, for he was a helpful sort of a wizard. "Why don't you go home and write down every single thing that you're worried about, and I'll make sure that none of these things ever happen."

He smiled.

"And then you won't have anything to worry about, will you?"

Mr Worry smiled.

It was the first time he'd smiled in a long time.

In fact, it was the first time he'd smiled that year.

He hurried home in great excitement.

When he got home, he sat down to write out all the things that worried him.

Every single thing.

It was a long list!

And then he went to bed, and had the best night's sleep he'd had in years.

The following morning, the wizard came round to collect Mr Worry's list.

"My goodness me," he said when he saw the size of it.

"However," he said, "leave it to me. I'll go off and make sure that none of these things ever happen."

And off he went.

"Nothing to worry about now," he called over his shoulder. "Nothing at all!"

Mr Worry heaved a sigh of relief.

That day was the first day in Mr Worry's life that he didn't have a single thing to worry about.

And the next day.

And the day after.

And the day after that.

On Monday, Tuesday, Wednesday, Thursday, Friday, Saturday and Sunday, Mr Worry didn't have a care in the world.

But ...

… on Monday morning he was a worried man.

Oh dear.

What do you think was worrying him?

Can you guess?

He went to see the wizard.

"Oh dear," said the wizard when he saw him standing on his doorstep. "What's worrying you?"

"I'll tell you," said Mr Worry.

"I'm worried because I don't have anything to worry about!"

And he went home.

To worry about not having anything to worry about!

THE END

MR.QUIET

by Roger Hargreaves

Mr Quiet liked the quiet life.

He lived, quietly, in a small little cottage in the middle of a wood.

The problem was, that small little cottage was in the middle of a wood in the middle of a country called Loudland!

Everything and everybody in Loudland was noisy.

Oh, the noise!

Dogs didn't go "woof" like dogs you know.

They went (take a deep breath) "WOOF!"

People didn't shut their doors like you or I would shut our doors.
They slammed them.

BANG!

People didn't talk to each other.

They shouted at each other.

"HELLO," they'd shout as they met in the street.

And, you've heard about something being as quiet as a mouse, haven't you?

Not in Loudland. They had the noisiest mice in the world.

"SQUEAK! SQUEAK!" they'd roar at each other.

Mr Noisy would have liked living in Loudland.

He'd have loved it.

But Mr Quiet didn't.

Noise frightened him.

So, he stayed in his cottage in the middle of his wood as much as he could.

But of course he couldn't stay there all the time.

Every week, for instance, he had to go shopping.

He used to creep into the grocer's shop.

"GOOD MORNING," bellowed the grocer. "WHAT CAN I DO FOR YOU?"

"Please," whispered Mr Quiet, "could I have some cornflakes, please?"

"WHAT?"

"Cornflakes. Please," he whispered.

"SPEAK UP!"

Mr Quiet tried his loudest whisper.

"Cornflakes."

"CAN'T HEAR YOU," shouted the grocer. "NEXT PLEASE!"

And poor Mr Quiet had to creep away without any cornflakes.

It wasn't fair, was it?

He crept into the butcher's.

"Please," he whispered, "I'd like some meat."

The butcher didn't even hear him.

He was humming to himself, loudly and fiercely.

Mr Quiet tried again.

"Please," he whispered, "I'd like some meat."

The butcher started to whistle.

It sounded more like a burglar alarm than a whistle.

Mr Quiet fled.

Empty-handed.

It often happened, which probably explains why he was so little.

Poor Mr Quiet.

He sat at home that night with a feeling of despair.

"Whatever am I to do?" he thought.

"It's no use," he thought. "I'll just have to try again."

And so, the following day, he went shopping again.

But, the same thing happened.

"CAN'T HEAR YOU," thundered the grocer.
"NEXT PLEASE!"

"CAN'T HEAR YOU," bellowed the greengrocer. "NEXT PLEASE!"

"CAN'T HEAR YOU," roared the milkman.
"NEXT PLEASE!"

"CAN'T HEAR YOU," boomed the butcher.
"NEXT PLEASE!"

Oh dear!

Poor Mr Quiet went home and went to bed.

Hungry.

The next morning, he was awakened by a noise which sounded like bombs dropping.

It was the Loudland postman knocking at Mr Quiet's door.

BANG! BANG! BANG! BANG!

Mr Quiet went and opened the door.

"MORNING," shouted the postman. "LETTER FOR YOU!"

Mr Quiet took the letter into his kitchen.

He sat down to open it.

He waited until the noise of the postman's footsteps died away.

CLUMP CLUMP CLUMP CLUMP clump clump.

Mr Quiet opened the letter in great excitement.

He'd never had a letter before.

It was from Mr Happy in Happyland.

An invitation!

To stay!

Mr Quiet was overjoyed.

He rushed upstairs and packed his bag and set off that very morning.

It was late when he arrived on Mr Happy's doorstep.

He knocked on Mr Happy's door.

Tap tap tap.

Mr Happy opened the door.

"Hello," he smiled. "I thought I heard something. You must be Mr Quiet. Well, don't just stand there, come in and have some supper."

It was the first proper meal Mr Quiet had had for months. And while he was eating it, he told Mr Happy all about the problems he'd been having in Loudland.

Mr Happy was most sympathetic.

Over breakfast the following morning, Mr Happy told Mr Quiet that he'd been thinking about his problem.

"I think," he said, "that under the circumstances you'd better stay here in Happyland." Mr Quiet's face lit up.

"And," continued Mr Happy, "we'll find you a house, and," he went on, "a job."

Mr Quiet's face dropped. "I'm not very good at jobs," he confessed, "because I'm too quiet."

"Ah," smiled Mr Happy. "I have the very job for a quiet chap like you!"

And so, the very next day, Mr Quiet started work. And he loves it.

Do you know where he works?

In the Happy Lending Library!

As you know, everybody who goes into a library has to be very quiet, and only whispering is allowed.

What a clever idea of Mr Happy's, wasn't it?

And these days Mr Quiet is as happy as can be.

Why, only the other day, do you know what he did on his way home from work? book?

He was so happy he laughed out loud.

Can you imagine?

Tee hee hee!

"NEXT PLEASE!"

THE END

MR.MUDDLE

by Roger Hargreaves

Poor Mr Muddle just couldn't get anything right.

Everything he did, everything he tried, everything he said was muddled.

Totally, utterly, completely, absolutely muddled!

Imagine, for instance, something as simple as hammering a nail into a wall.

Now what could get muddled with hammering a nail into a wall?

Mr Muddle could get it muddled!

And frequently did!

Imagine, for instance, something as simple as putting on your coat.

Now what could get muddled with putting on your coat?

Well, see for yourself.

Only Mr Muddle would put on his coat like that!

Imagine, for instance, something as simple as going for a walk.

Now what could get muddled with going for a walk?

Well, when your legs start walking one way and you start walking the other, that's a very muddly sort of a walk.

Poor Mr Muddle, walking one way and going another!

Now, you'd probably like to know where Mr Muddle lives.

In a house by the sea near a place called Seatown.

Mr Muddle's house was supposed to be in the country, but Mr Muddle (who built the house himself) had got the place muddled up!

Of course!

And you can tell that Mr Muddle had built the house himself, can't you?

This story starts one afternoon when Mr Muddle was having his breakfast.

Yes, we know you don't have breakfast in the afternoon, but you do if you get your mealtimes muddled up.

Mr Muddle was having bread and butter and jam and a cup of tea with milk and sugar.

He spread the butter on the table, and then spread the jam on the plate, and then poured the milk on the bread, and then filled the cup with sugar, and then poured the tea on the bread!

What a terrible muddly mixed-up breakfast!

That afternoon, after breakfast, he went for a walk down the beach near his house in order to work up an appetite for supper.

He met an old fisherman called George, whom he knew quite well.

"Good afternoon, Mr Muddle," said George.

"Good evening," replied Mr Muddle.

George smiled. "How would you like to come fishing with me?" he asked.

"Ooo, no please," replied Mr Muddle, eagerly.

"Help me push the boat out from the beach," called George.

"Rightho," said Mr Muddle, and pulled the boat further up on to the beach.

"Oh, Mr Muddle," said George, and he had to show Mr Muddle the difference between pulling and pushing.

However, eventually, somehow or other, they managed to get the boat out to sea.

"Now let's fish," said George, dropping a fishing line over the side of the boat.

"Rightho," said Mr Muddle, and dropped himself over the side of the boat!

SPLASH!

"Oh, Mr Muddle," said George, again.

It wasn't any good, and they didn't catch any fish, and so they decided to go home before it became dark.

"Help me pull the boat up on to the beach," called George.

"Rightho," said Mr Muddle, and pushed the boat back into the water.

George was just about to say "Oh, Mr Muddle" again, when he had an idea.

He smiled to himself.

"Help me push the boat out into the sea," George called.

"Rightho," said Mr Muddle, and pulled the boat up on to the beach!

"Well done, Mr Muddle," said George.

Mr Muddle smiled a smile and went home.

George smiled a smile and went to tell everybody.

The following day, in Seatown, Mr Brick the builder asked Mr Muddle to hold his coat for him.

"Rightho," said Mr Muddle, and held his ladder for him – which is what Mr Brick really wanted.

"Well done, Mr Muddle," smiled Mr Brick, who'd been talking to George.

Mr Muddle was very pleased.

Then Mrs Scrub at the laundry asked Mr Muddle to pass her the soap.

"Rightho," said Mr Muddle, and passed her a clothes peg – which is what Mrs Scrub really wanted.

"Well done, Mr Muddle," smiled Mrs Scrub, who'd also been talking to George.

Mr Muddle was extremely pleased.

And then Mr Black the coalman asked Mr Muddle to lift a sack of coal down from his lorry.

"Rightho," said Mr Muddle, and lifted a sack of coal up on to the lorry – which is what Mr Black had wanted all along.

"Well done, Mr Muddle," smiled Mr Black.

George had talked to everybody!

Mr Muddle was delighted.

In fact, Mr Muddle was so delighted he decided to go home and cook himself a large meal to celebrate.

Roast turkey, and peas, and potatoes, and gravy!

He put the turkey in the cupboard to cook!

He peeled the peas!

He put the potatoes in the refrigerator to boil!

And then do you know what he did?

He tried to slice the gravy!!

Oh, Mr Muddle!

THE END

MR.BOUNCE

by Roger Hargreaves

Mr Bounce was very small and like a rubber ball.

He just couldn't keep himself on the ground!

He bounced all over the place!

And, as you can imagine, that made things rather difficult.

Last week, for instance, Mr Bounce was out walking when he came to a farm.

He climbed over the farm gate, and you can guess what happened next, can't you?

He jumped down from the gate, and …

After he had picked himself up, Mr Bounce went into his living room and sat down to think.

BOUNCE!

Mr Bounce bounced off the chair and banged his head on the ceiling.

BANG! went Mr Bounce's head on the ceiling.

"OUCH!" said Mr Bounce.

"This is ridiculous," Mr Bounce thought to himself, rubbing his head. "I must do something to stop all this bouncing about."

He thought and thought.

"I know," he thought. "I'll go and see the doctor!"

So, after breakfast, Mr Bounce set off to the nearest town to see the doctor.

He was passing a tennis court when he tripped over a pebble.

BOUNCE! he bounced.

And he bounced right on to the court where two children were playing tennis, and you can guess what happened next, can't you?

The children didn't realise that Mr Bounce wasn't a tennis ball, and started hitting him with their tennis racquets backwards and forwards over the net.

BOUNCE!

"OOO!"

BOUNCE!

"OW!"

BOUNCE!

"OUCH!"

Poor Mr Bounce.

Eventually, one of the children hit Mr Bounce so hard he bounced right out of the tennis court.

Mr Bounce bounced off down the road towards the town.

"Oh dear," he said, feeling very sorry for himself. "I've been bounced black and blue!"

A bus was coming along the road, and Mr Bounce decided that the safest place for him to be would be on it.

He got on and sat down, still feeling more than a little sorry for himself.

The bus drove into town.

The bus stopped right outside the doctor's.

Mr Bounce stepped down from the bus.

And you can guess what happened next, can't you?

He didn't step down on to the pavement outside the doctor's. Oh no, not Mr Bounce!

He stepped off the bus, and on to the pavement, and bounced – in through the doctor's window!

Doctor Makeyouwell was sitting at his desk, enjoying his mid-morning cup of coffee.

Mr Bounce sailed through the open window, and landed …

Well, you can guess where he landed, can't you?

That's right!

SPLASH! went the coffee.

"OUCH!" squeaked Mr Bounce. The coffee was rather hot.

"Good heavens!" exclaimed Doctor Makeyouwell.

After the doctor had fished Mr Bounce out of his coffee, and sat him on some blotting paper to dry out, he listened to what Mr Bounce had to tell him.

"So you see," said Mr Bounce finally, "you must give me something to stop me bouncing about all over the place quite so much."

"Hmmm," pondered the doctor.

After some thought, Doctor Makeyouwell went to his medicine cabinet and took out a pair of tiny red boots.

"This should do the trick," he told Mr Bounce. "Heavy boots! That should stop the bouncing!"

"Oh thank you, Doctor Makeyouwell," said Mr Bounce, and he walked home wearing his red boots.

Not bounced!

Walked!

That night, Mr Bounce went to bed wearing his heavy boots.

And then he went to sleep.

The following morning, he woke up and yawned and stretched, and bounced out of bed.

And can you guess what happened next?

No, he didn't bounce down the stairs.

He went straight through the bedroom floorboards, and finished up in the kitchen!

THE END

MR.SLOW

by Roger Hargreaves

Mr Slow, as you might well know, or maybe you don't, lived next door to Mr Busy.

He'd built his house himself.

Slowly.

It had taken him ten years!

And, as you might well know, or maybe you don't, Mr Slow talked in an extraordinarily slow way.

He … talked … like … this.

And every single thing he did was as slow as the way he talked.

For instance.

If Mr Slow was writing this book about himself, you wouldn't be able to read it yet.

He wouldn't even have got as far as this page!

For instance.

If Mr Slow was eating a currant cake for tea, it took him until bedtime.

He'd eat it crumb by crumb, currant by currant, chewing each crumb and each currant one hundred times.

For instance.

Last Christmas, it took Mr Slow until New Year's Day
to open his Christmas presents.

And then it took him until Easter to write his thank-you letters!

Oh, he was a slow man.

Now, this story isn't about the time Mr Slow went on a picnic with Mr Busy.

That's another story.

No, this story is about the time Mr Slow decided to get a job.

He read all the job advertisements in the Sunday paper (which took him until Wednesday), and then he went and got himself a job reading the news on television.

Can you imagine?

It was very embarrassing!

"Good … evening …," said Mr Slow. "Here … is … the … nine … o' … clock … news."

It took him until midnight to read it!

And everybody who was watching went to sleep.

So, that job wasn't any good.

Was it?

Then, Mr Slow got himself a job as a taxi driver.

"Take me to the railway station," cried Mr Uppity, as he leapt into his taxi. "I have a train to catch at three o'clock!"

"Right ... ho," said Mr Slow, and set off.

At one mile an hour!

And arrived at the station at four o'clock.

So, that job wasn't any good.

Was it?

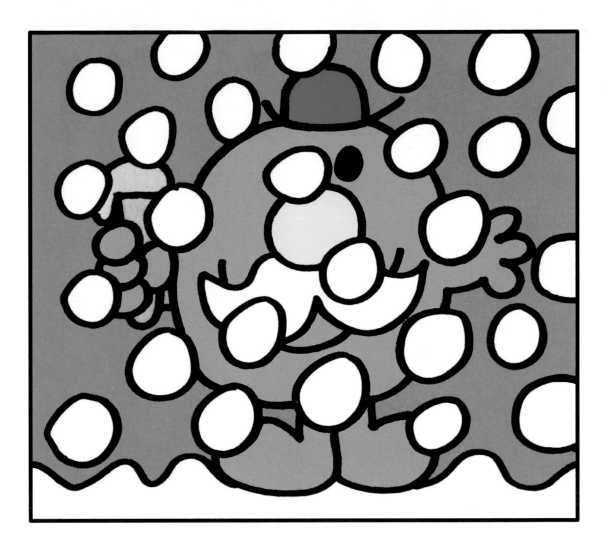

And, that summer, Mr Slow got a job making ice cream. But, by the time he'd made the ice cream, it wasn't exactly the right sort of weather to be selling ice cream!

Brrrr!

So, Mr Slow got himself a job making woolly scarves. But, by the time he'd finished making the scarves, it wasn't exactly the right sort of weather to be selling scarves!

Phew!

Poor Mr Slow.

He went around to ask the other Mr Men what he should do.

"Be a racing driver!" suggested Mr Silly.

Can you imagine?

No!

"Be an engine driver!" suggested Mr Funny.

Can you imagine?

No! No!

"Be a speedboat driver!" suggested Mr Tickle.

Can you imagine?

No! No! No!

But then, Mr Happy had an extremely good idea.

Most sensible.

"Be a steamroller driver," he suggested.

And today that is exactly what Mr Slow does.

Slowly backwards and slowly forwards he drives.

Up and down.

Down and up.

Ever so slowly.

The next time you see a steamroller doing that, look and see if Mr Slow is driving it.

If he is, you shout to him, "Hello, Mr Slow! Are you having a nice time?"

And he'll wave, and shout back to you.

"Yes … thank … you … Good … bye!"

THE END

MR.LAZY

by Roger Hargreaves

Mr Lazy lives in Sleepyland, which is a very lazy-looking and sleepy-like place.

The birds in Sleepyland fly so slowly they sometimes fall out of the sky.

The grass takes so long to grow it only needs cutting once a year.

Even the trees are lazy-looking and sleepy-like.

And do you know what time everybody gets up in Sleepyland?

The answer is, they don't get up in the morning.

They get up in the afternoon!

And, incidentally, this is what a Sleepyland clock looks like.

Everything takes so long to do there's only time for four hours a day!

Anyway, this story starts with Mr Lazy being fast asleep in bed. In Sleepyland they call that being slow asleep!

He spends rather a lot of time in bed. It's his favourite place to be!

He opened his eyes, yawned, yawned again – and went back to sleep.

Later, Mr Lazy opened his eyes again, yawned, yawned again, and went back to sleep again.

Much later, Mr Lazy got up and went to make his breakfast.

We say breakfast, although really it was teatime.

He put the kettle on to make some tea. Kettles take two hours to boil in Sleepyland!

Then he toasted a slice of bread. Bread takes three hours to go brown in Sleepyland.

Toast never gets burnt there!

While he was waiting for his kettle to boil and his bread to toast, Mr Lazy went into the garden of Yawn Cottage – which was where he lived.

He sat down on a chair. And you can probably guess what happened next.

That's right. He yawned, and yawned again, and went to sleep.

Suddenly, he woke up with a jump, which is something that doesn't happen very often to Mr Lazy.

And the reason he woke up with a jump was because of the noise.

"WAKE UP," said the noise.

"WAKEUPWAKEUPWAKEUP."

There were two men standing in front of him.

"I'm Mr Busy," said one of the men.

"And I'm Mr Bustle," said the other.

"Come along now," said Mr Bustle busily.

"We can't have you sleeping all day," added Mr Busy, bustling Mr Lazy to his feet.

"But who are you?" asked Mr Lazy.

"We're Bustle and Busy," they replied.

"Oh," said Mr Lazy.

"Come along now," said Mr Busy, "we haven't got all day."

"But …" said Mr Lazy.

"No time for buts," said Mr Busy. "Or ifs," added Mr Bustle.

"There's the wood to chop and the beds to make and the floors to clean and the coal to get and the windows to polish and the plates to wash and the furniture to dust and the grass to cut and the hedges to clip and the food to cook!"

"And the clothes to mend," added Mr Busy.

"Oh dear," groaned Mr Lazy in a daze. "The wood to clean and the beds to get and the floors to cut and the coal to cook and the windows to make and the plates to mend and the furniture to chop and the grass to wash and the hedges to dust and the clothes to clip?"

He'd got it all completely wrong he was in such a daze.

Then Bustle and Busy set Mr Lazy to work.

Chopping and making and cleaning and getting and polishing and washing and dusting and cutting and clipping and cooking and mending.

Not to mention all the fetching and carrying!

Poor Mr Lazy!

"Now," they said when he'd finished, "it's time for a walk!"

And off they set on the longest walk Mr Lazy had ever been on.

Mr Lazy is one of those people who never walks when he has a chance of sitting down, and never sits down when he has a chance of lying down.

But this day he had no choice. They made him walk for miles and miles and miles, until he felt his legs must be worn right down to his body.

Poor Mr Lazy!

When they arrived back at Yawn Cottage, Mr Busy said, "Right! Now for a run!"

"Oh no," groaned Mr Lazy.

"When I blow this whistle," said Mr Bustle, producing a whistle, "you've got to start running."

"As fast as you can," added Mr Busy.

Mr Lazy groaned a deep groan, and closed his eyes.

Mr Bustle put the whistle to his lips.

"Wheeeeeeeeeeeeee," whistled the whistle.

"Wheeeeeeeeeeeeeeeeee," went the whistle.

Mr Lazy, poor Mr Lazy, started to run.

But his legs weren't getting him anywhere.

He opened his eyes and looked down to see why.

And the reason his legs weren't getting him anywhere was because he was sitting on a chair in the garden.

And there was no sign of Mr Busy and Mr Bustle!

It had all been a terrible dream!

And the whistle was the whistling kettle boiling in the kitchen!

Mr Lazy heaved a sigh of relief.

And then he went into the kitchen, and sat down to have his breakfast, and to think about his dream.

But you know what happened next, don't you?

"Wake up, Mr Lazy!"

"WAKEUPWAKEUPWAKEUP!"

THE END

MR.MESSY

by Roger Hargreaves

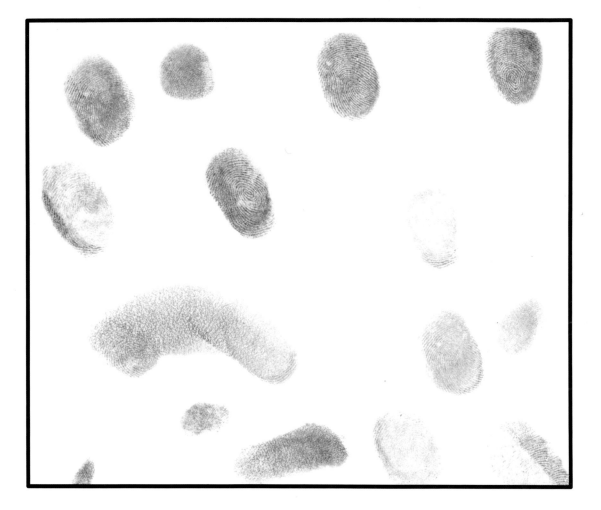

Mr Messy was the messiest person you've ever met in your whole life.

He looked messy because he was messy, in everything he did.

You could always tell where Mr Messy had been because he left a trail of messy fingerprints wherever he'd been.

Oh yes, Mr Messy was messy by name, messy by nature!

Mr Messy lived in a particularly messy-looking house.

The paint was peeling.

The windows were broken.

There were tiles missing from the roof.

The flower beds were overgrown with weeds.

The garden gate was off its hinges.

And had Mr Messy cut the grass in his garden lately?

He had not!

One morning, Mr Messy woke up in his messy bed, yawned, scratched, got up, cleaned his teeth (leaving the top off the toothpaste), had his breakfast (spilling cornflakes all over the floor), and then set out for a walk (tripping over a brush he'd left lying in the garden two weeks before).

There was a wood behind Mr Messy's messy house with the messy garden, and that's where he went for his walk.

It was a particularly large wood with lots and lots of trees and it took Mr Messy a long time to walk through it. But he didn't really mind because he felt like walking that morning.

So he walked and walked right through the wood until he came to the other side.

And do you know what he found on the other side of the wood?

Mr Messy found the neatest, prettiest-looking little cottage that he had ever seen.

It had a lovely little garden with a stream running through the middle of it.

There was a man in the garden, clipping the hedge.

He looked up as Mr Messy approached.

"Good morning! I'm Mr Messy!" said Mr Messy.

"I can see that," replied the man, looking him up and down. "I'm Mr Tidy."

"And I'm Mr Neat," said another man, appearing out of the house.

"Tidy and Neat," said Mr Tidy.

"Neat and Tidy," said Mr Neat.

"We're in business together," explained Mr Tidy. "And the people who own this house have asked us to do some work for them."

"What sort of work?" asked Mr Messy.

"Oh, we make things nice and neat," said Mr Neat.

"Tidy things up," added Mr Tidy.

"Perhaps we could come along and do some work for you?" said Mr Neat, looking at Mr Messy, who was looking even messier than usual that particular morning.

"But, I don't want things neat and tidy," said Mr Messy, looking downright miserable at the thought of it.

"Nonsense!" said Mr Tidy.

"Fiddlesticks!" said Mr Neat.

"But," said Mr Messy.

"Come along," said Mr Neat.

"Off we go," said Mr Tidy.

"But, but …" said Mr Messy.

"But nothing," said Mr Neat and, bundling him into their van, which was parked behind the house, off they went to Mr Messy's house at the other side of the wood.

"Good heavens!" said Mr Neat when he saw where Mr Messy lived.

"Good gracious!" added Mr Tidy.

"This is the messiest house I have ever seen in all my born days," they both said together at the same time.

"Better do something about it," said Mr Neat.

And before Mr Messy could open his mouth, the two of them were rushing here and there about Mr Messy's house.

Mr Neat hoed

and mowed

and pruned

and snipped

and clipped

and cleared

and dug

and made the garden look neater than it had ever looked before.

Mr Tidy cleaned

and primed

and rubbed

and painted

and mended

and made the outside of Mr Messy's house look tidier than it had ever looked before.

Then they both went inside the house.

"Good heavens!" said Mr Neat for the second time that morning.

"Good gracious!" said Mr Tidy for the second time that morning.

And then they set about cleaning the house from top to bottom.

They brushed and swept and polished and scrubbed and made the inside of the house look neater and tidier than it had ever looked before.

"There we are," said Mr Tidy.

"All finished," said Mr Neat.

"Tidy and neat," said Mr Tidy.

"Neat and tidy," said Mr Neat.

Mr Messy just didn't know what to say.

Then they both looked at Mr Messy.

"Are you thinking what I'm thinking?" Mr Neat said to Mr Tidy.

"Precisely," replied Mr Tidy.

"What we're both thinking," they said together to Mr Messy, "is that you look much too messy to live in a neat and tidy house like this!"

"But ..." said Mr Messy.

But whatever Mr Messy said was no use, and Mr Neat and Mr Tidy whisked him off to the bathroom upstairs.

It had been the messiest room in the house, but now of course it was neat as a new pin.

Then Mr Neat got hold of one of Mr Messy's arms, and Mr Tidy got hold of the other arm, and they picked him up and put him straight into the bath.

Mr Messy wasn't used to having baths!

Mr Neat and Mr Tidy washed

and brushed

and cleaned

and scrubbed

and combed Mr Messy until he didn't look like Mr Messy at all.

In fact he looked the opposite of messy!

He looked at himself in the mirror.

"You know what I'm going to have to do now?" he said in a rather fierce voice.

Mr Neat and Mr Tidy looked worried.

"What are you going to have to do?" they asked Mr Messy.

"I'm going to have to change my name!" said Mr Messy.

And then he chuckled.

And Mr Neat and Mr Tidy chuckled.

And then Mr Messy laughed.

And Mr Neat and Mr Tidy laughed.

And then they all laughed together, and became the best of friends.

And that really is the end of the story, except to say that if you're a messy sort of a person, you might have a visit from two people.

And you know what they are called, don't you?

THE END

MR.BUSY

by Roger Hargreaves

There has never been anybody quite like Mr Busy.

He could do things ten times as fast as ever you or I could.

For instance, if he was reading this book, he'd have finished it by now.

He lived in a very busy-looking house which he'd built himself.

As you can see.

It had lots of doors and windows, and do you know what it was called?

Weekend Cottage!

Do you know why?

Because that's how long it took him to build it!

One fine summer morning, Mr Busy was up and about bright and early at six o'clock.

He jumped out of bed, and had a bath, and cleaned his teeth, and cooked his breakfast, and ate his breakfast, and read the paper, and washed up, and made his bed, and cleaned the house from top to bottom.

By which time it was seven o'clock.

Busy Mr Busy!

Now, next door to Mr Busy lived somebody who wasn't quite such a busy person.

In fact, he was a very unbusy person.

Mr Slow!

If he was reading this book he'd … read … it … like … this!

He'd still be on the first page!

And that same fine summer morning, at five past seven, when Mr Busy knocked at his door, Mr Slow was fast asleep in bed.

He'd gone to bed for an afternoon nap the day before, and somehow hadn't woken up until he heard Mr Busy knocking at his door.

"Who's … that … knocking … at … my … door?"
he called downstairs.

"Good morning," cried Mr Busy. "Can I come in?"

And, without waiting for an answer, he went inside.

"Where are you?" he called.

"Up … stairs," came the slow reply.

So Mr Busy went upstairs, two at a time.

"Good heavens!" he said. "You're still in bed!"

And he made Mr Slow get up.

And he made his bed for him, and cooked his breakfast for him, and cleaned his house for him.

Poor Mr Slow.

He hated to be rushed and fussed.

"Right," said Mr Busy briskly. "It's a fine day. Let's go for a picnic."

Mr Slow pulled a face.

"I … don't … like … picnics," he complained.

"Nonsense," replied Mr Busy, and busied himself around Mr Slow's kitchen making up a picnic for the two of them.

It took him a minute and a half.

"Right," he cried when he'd finished. "Off we go!"

And he bustled Mr Slow out of his front door, and off they set.

As you can imagine, Mr Busy walks extremely quickly.

And, as you can imagine, Mr Slow doesn't.

So, by the time Mr Busy had walked a mile, do you know how far Mr Slow had walked?

To his own garden gate!

Mr Busy hurried back.

"Come on," he cried impatiently. "Hurry up!"

"Hurry … up?" replied Mr Slow.

"Im … poss … i … ble!"

"Oh, all right," said Mr Busy. "We'll have a picnic in your garden."

"Wait a minute, though," he added. "The grass needs cutting."

And he rushed back to Weekend Cottage and rushed back again with his lawnmower, and rushed up and down cutting Mr Slow's lawn.

It took him two and a half minutes!

It would have taken him two minutes, but he had to mow around Mr Slow, who couldn't get out of the way in time.

"Right!" said Mr Busy. "Picnic time!"

And together on that fine summer day they had a fine picnic.

Well, actually, Mr Busy had a finer picnic than Mr Slow because he ate more quickly and had most of the food.

Mr Busy stretched out on the grass.

"That was fun," he said. "I like picnics!"

"You … do! … I … don't," said Mr Slow.

"Tell you what," went on Mr Busy, ignoring him. "Tomorrow we'll go on a proper picnic, out in the country."

Mr Slow pulled a face.

"And," went on Mr Busy, "in order to do that and get you out into the country, I'll have to call for you earlier than I did this morning."

Mr Slow pulled another face.

"See you tomorrow then," said Mr Busy, and went home and cleaned his house from bottom to top.

The following morning, Mr Busy jumped out of bed at five o'clock, and had a bath, and cleaned his teeth, and cooked his breakfast, and ate his breakfast, and read the paper, and washed up, and made his bed, and cleaned the house from top to bottom.

By which time it was six o'clock.

He went and knocked on Mr Slow's front door.

"Come on! Come on!" he cried. "Time to be up and about! Picnic day!"

No reply.

"Come on!" cried Mr Busy again.

No reply.

Mr Busy went inside.

And went upstairs, three at a time, and into Mr Slow's bedroom, expecting to find him in bed.

But he wasn't.

And he wasn't anywhere upstairs.

And he wasn't anywhere downstairs.

"Bother," said Mr Busy. "I wonder where he's got to?"

Where Mr Slow had got to was under his bed.

Hiding!

He didn't want to go on any picnic.

Not he.

"Bother," said Mr Busy again. "That means I'll have to go on a picnic on my own!"

Under his bed, Mr Slow smiled a slow smile.

"What … a … good … idea," he said.

And went to sleep.

Snoring very slowly.

THE END

MR.WRONG

by Roger Hargreaves

Whatever Mr Wrong did was absolutely, totally, completely, utterly wrong.

However hard he tried, he just couldn't do anything right.

Just look at his house!

One fine morning, Mr Wrong woke up.

He hadn't slept very well because of the way he'd made his bed the day before.

He jumped out of bed, fell over (twice), put on his shoes (on the wrong feet), went to the bathroom (tripping over the bathmat), squeezed out some toothpaste (on to the wrong side of his toothbrush), cleaned his teeth (ouch), and went downstairs.

Bump, bump, bump, bump, bump, bump, bump!

Not a very good start to the day.

In fact, his usual wrong start to the day.

In his kitchen, Mr Wrong poured some milk onto his cornflakes.

And missed!

As he sat in his kitchen, that fine morning, eating his dry cornflakes, he sighed.

"Oh dear," he thought, "I do so wish that everything I do wasn't quite so absolutely, totally, completely, utterly wrong."

So, after breakfast, he went for a walk in order to think how he could solve his problem.

It took him ten minutes to get out of the house, because he kept trying to open his front door outwards instead of inwards!

As he walked along, he passed a worm.

"Good morning, Dog," he said.

The worm grinned.

He was used to Mr Wrong.

He met a postman.

"Good morning, Mr Wrong," called the postman cheerfully.

"Good morning, Doctor," replied Mr Wrong.

Oh dear!

He met old Mrs Twinkle, who lived down the lane.

"Good morning, Mr Wrong," she smiled.

"Good morning, Mr Twinkle," replied Mr Wrong.

Oh dear!

And then he met somebody he'd never met before.

Somebody who sort of looked like him, but didn't.

"Good morning, Sir," said that somebody.

"Good morning, Madam," replied Mr Wrong. "I'm Mr Wrong."

"I guessed that," replied the person. "Well, I'm Mr Right."

"Now tell me," he went on, "why are you walking along looking so miserable?"

"Because," replied Mr Wrong, "I can't do anything right!"

"In which case," said Mr Right, "we'd better do something about it. Follow me."

And off he set.

And off set Mr Wrong.

In the opposite direction!

Mr Right hurried back, and turned him round.

"This way," he said, and they walked together to where Mr Right lived.

It was a house which somehow looked something like Mr Wrong's house.

But different.

Mr Right took Mr Wrong into his living room.

"I think," he said, "that the only way you are ever going to change is for you to come and live with me for a while, and you may end up being not quite so absolutely, totally, completely, utterly wrong about everything."

"Sit down," he said, "and we'll talk about it."

Mr Wrong sat down.

And missed!

Mr Wrong stayed with Mr Right for a month.

And, during that time, he changed.

After one week, he was slightly less wrong than he had been before.

After two weeks, he was even more slightly less wrong than he had been before.

And, after a whole four weeks, he was a changed Mr Man.

You could hardly tell the difference between him and Mr Right.

Don't you agree?

Mr Right was delighted.

"Told you," he cried. "Told you that everything about you might end up being not quite so absolutely, totally, completely, utterly wrong!"

"In fact," he continued, "you've really turned out all right!"

Mr Wrong blushed.

It was quite the nicest thing anyone had ever said to him in the whole of his life.

And he went home.

And lived happily, and right, ever after.

Now.

You probably think that's the end of the story. Don't you?

Well, it isn't!

And the reason it isn't is because of what happened to Mr Right.

The trouble was, you see, that the longer Mr Wrong had stayed with Mr Right, and the more right Mr Wrong became, the more wrong Mr Right had become.

Isn't that extraordinary?

"Oh dear," Mr Right sighed. "My plan didn't quite work out the way I'd planned it after all."

And he went to bed.

In the bath!

THE END

Mr. Bounce

Mr. Messy